MW00896618

Magnificently You

Copyright © 2021 L.S. Kudzin
All rights reserved.

To all of my little men out there, always remember, even when this world tells you otherwise, that YOU are magnificent.

You are magnificently you, little guy, and it ain't no lie. You shine like the stars high above in the sky. Always remember, be all that you can, for one of these days you'll be a mighty man.

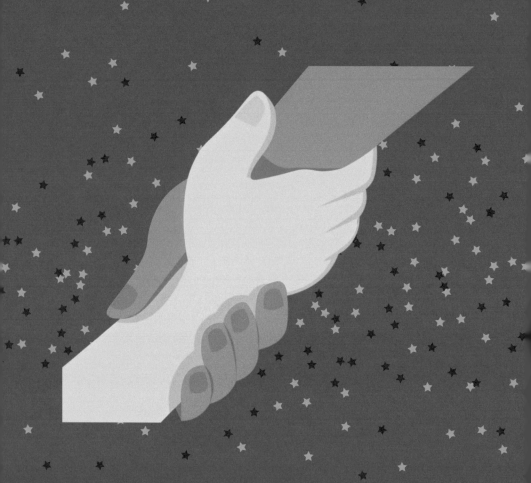

Mindful of others, good deeds will go far. You help those in need, you're a superstar!

Amazing and kind to people you meet,
from the richest of rich, down to those
on the street.

Gentle and loving to family and friends, be careful with words, try not to offend.

8

Noble, head high, with your shoulders held back. Stand tall little man, there is nothing you lack.

Imaginative, folks are inspired its
true. Don't be shy little guy, be you,
aim for the sky.

Fearless, don't be afraid to try, be
brave and be bold right on down to
your soul.

12

Intelligent, you know it's cool to be smart, no shame, don't refrain, go ahead flex that brain.

Charming, you chase away gloom, your smile
brightens rooms. Let your light shine forth, you
know your true worth.

Excellence you'll accept nothing less,
you expect it from life, you deserve
only the best.

Noteable, you are worthy of esteem.
Remarkable you, you're admirable,
indeed.

19

Treasured, you are adored my sweet, from the top of your head, right on down to your feet.

My dear boy, you are wonderful it's
true. There's no one on earth who's
exactly like you!

Made in the USA
Thornton, CO
03/03/24 15:26:20

271cdc8a-9f60-4e46-aac0-99c72f43ff97R01